WELCOME TO
FURTOPIA

Copyright © 2021 by Hollan Publishing, Inc.

Animal Crossing® and Animal Crossing: New Horizons® are trademarks of Nintendo.

The Animal Crossing and Animal Crossing: New Horizons games are copyright © Nintendo.

Sky Pony Press books may be purchased in bulk at special discounts for sales promotion, corporate gifts, fund-raising, or educational purposes. Special editions can also be created to specifications. For details, contact the Special Sales Department, Sky Pony Press, 307 West 36th Street, 11th Floor, New York, NY 10018 or info@skyhorsepublishing.com.

Sky Pony® is a registered trademark of Skyhorse Publishing, Inc.®, a Delaware corporation.

Visit our website at www.skyponypress.com.

10 9 8 7 6 5 4 3 2 1

Cover design by Kai Texel
Cover artwork by Grace Sandford

Print ISBN: 978-1-5107-6527-6
E-Book ISBN: 978-1-5107-6581-8

Printed in the United States of America

ISLAND ADVENTURES
WELCOME TO
FURTOPIA
BOOK 1

AN UNOFFICIAL NOVEL FOR FANS OF ANIMAL CROSSING

WINTER MORGAN

Sky Pony Press
New York

TABLE OF CONTENTS

CHAPTER 1

EVERY DAY IS THE SAME

Alana lived on the same block her entire life. She knew all her neighbors and the secret hiding spots in her backyard, which made her the reigning hide-and-seek champion of Cranberry Lane when she was younger. Although she enjoyed playing with her friends, she yearned to go on a real adventure like the ones she read about in books. Every night before bed, she created her own incredible tales. Alana wrote stories about people who traveled to outer space, climbed mountains, or lived in different countries across the globe. She imagined what her life would be like if she were able to live out an adventure. Despite reading how-to guides on how to survive in the wild or at sea, her real life never gave her a chance to try out these skills. It was very predictable

Every morning her mother made oatmeal with apples and cinnamon. Truthfully, Alana was a picky eater, and this was the only breakfast food she would eat, but even Alana was growing bored of having the same breakfast. In fact, Alana was bored a lot. She was bored of the PBJ sandwiches her mom made for lunch, and she was bored of homework. The only time Alana wasn't bored was when she played video games.

Alana's parents set a timer when she logged onto games, and when the buzzer went off, so did the screens. Alana always begged for extra time, but her parents never agreed to it.

"It's so much fun and it's the only time I'm not bored," she pleaded.

"Pick up a book," her mother said, as she shut down whatever electronic device Alana was using.

"I always read," said Alana. This was true, she was an avid reader, but she also liked creating her own worlds, and meeting new people in the games, which she couldn't do in books. Yes, she did write her own stories, but she loved creating new worlds in video games. She tried to explain this to her parents, but they didn't understand.

One day, while watching TV Alana saw an ad for a very unique island getaway where a kid could be transported through their TV to their very own island. She was excited. This sounded like a dream. The ad promised that participants would be able to develop this island all by themselves. They could plan the community, pick their own fruit, fish, and go on many adventures. Alana wanted to sign up right away. She called her mother over to the screen.

"Mom! Look at this island adventure." She stood by the TV screen and pointed to the ad she had paused with the remote control. She pressed play and watched the commercial alongside her mother. The commercial showed a little girl with red pigtails living in a small wooden cottage on a lush green island filled with red and purple flowers. She looked to be socializing with a chatty rabbit.

"I need to do this, Mom!" Alana declared, "It looks like so much fun. I can build my own island."

"Let me do some research," her mom responded, which was what she said when she was avoiding making a decision. Her mom said that a lot, and Alana believed her mom hoped Alana would either forget or change her mind before her mom had to make a decision.

"Let's research it together," Alana suggested.

"Okay, later." Her mother got up and walked toward the kitchen.

"Why can't we research it now?" Alana questioned.

"Let's do it another time."

"Don't you remember what it's like to be a kid? You don't get to make any decisions. If I go on this island adventure, I can have an island that's all my own. I can do something I've never done before and that is exciting."

Alana's mother paused. "Okay."

"Really?"

* * *

Alana's mother watched the ad a few times and pulled out her personal checklist of questions that she used when assessing if a video game was appropriate.

Violent? No. Dangerous? No. Creative? Yes. Teaches independence and strengthens motor skills? Yes.

"This is an educational game," Alana's mom said.

"Does that mean we get bonus points on your quiz?"

Alana's mother laughed. "It means I'm allowing you to take this island adventure." Her mother paused. "If you add making your bed each morning to your list of chores."

"Can I start it now?"

"It's bedtime," her mother reminded her. "You can go tomorrow."

"Can we watch the ad one more time?" she asked her mother.

"Sure."

They sat together on the plush blue couch and watched a racoon tell them about the sorts of adventures one might have on their own island. There would be new friends to meet, fishing tournaments, buried treasure to be unearthed, and balloons that flew through the sky carrying presents. Alana wanted to watch the commercial again, but her mother said it was time to go to sleep.

Alana raced into her bedroom. The sooner she crawled into bed, the sooner it would be morning and she could start her island adventure. She imagined the first thing she would do when she arrived on her island: She would jump into the water and go for a swim. She'd then eat all the fruit she could find on the luscious trees that filled the island. She also came up with a bunch of names for her island.

After she rattled off a bunch of potential names from Newfoundia to Fruitland, her mother walked into her room.

"You need to go to sleep," she said softly.

"I'm sorry. I'm just so excited for my island adventure. I was trying to think of a name for the island."

Alana clung to her stuffed teddy bear, Furry, that she'd had since she was little. She didn't remember naming the teddy bear because she was only a toddler at the time. She loved Furry the bear. As her mother closed Alana's bedroom door and wished her a good night, Alana came up with the perfect name for her island: Furtopia. Although she couldn't bring her beloved stuffed animal on the trip, she'd think of him every time she said the name of the island.

The minute the sun shone through Alana's window, she jumped out of bed and raced to the living room, where she turned on the TV and logged on to her island adventure.

Within seconds, she was transported out of her living room and standing in front of a ticket counter at an airport, where two adorable wide-eyed raccoons with pink ears stood behind the counter. The raccoons, who wore button down shirts emblazoned with the island adventure logo, introduced themselves.

"I'm Tick."

"I'm Tock."

"We're glad you signed up for this adventure," said Tick, and then he walked her to the gate where the plane was located. As she approached the plane's entrance, her heart started to beat rapidly.

She wasn't allowed to bring anything on this journey. For years, she had wondered what she would bring if she was ever going to be marooned on an island. She always thought it would be Furry the bear. Now that she was flying to a real deserted island, she realized she should have been more practical when making that type of decision. If she were allowed to bring something on this trip, it would have been food or a sleeping bag. She hoped she had the skills to acquire them once she reached the island.

As the plane took off, Alana looked out the window, wishing she had been able to bring Furry. It would have been nice to have brought one thing from home, but then she reminded herself that this was an adventure and also a new beginning. She couldn't focus on being back at home; she had to think about all the new friends she'd meet.

On the plane, she saw a video about what to expect once she arrived on the island. It reminded her of the commercial she had watched with her mother and that made her feel homesick again. The video showed scenes of the island in the snow, and Alana started to feel better as she imagined building a snowman or having a snowball fight with her new friends. The video inspired her to think of ways to set up her island. She couldn't believe she'd have her own property where she could spend lazy days lounging at the beach or taking long swims in the ocean. There were also pictures of people at parties on the island. She hoped she'd make new friends and throw a party. She couldn't believe how much she could do on the island, but then she reminded herself not to get carried away yet. She still had to build it.

Alana looked out the window while the plane descended toward the ground. She squinted as she attempted to figure out the landscape of the island. There were many rivers running through it, so Alana knew that she'd have to build a lot of bridges. It was going to be hard work, but she was up for the challenge. As the plane flew lower, she spotted a waterfall.

When the plane landed, Alana couldn't wait to unbuckle herself and rush toward the exit. Tick and Tock, the two raccoons from the ticket counter, led Alana off the seaplane and onto the pier.

"Welcome," they said in unison.

"I'm so excited to be here," Alana said as she looked past the racoons and surveyed the island filled with cherry trees. It was breezy. Alana's red pigtails waved about in the wind, and she pushed them out of her face. She could smell the salty ocean air.

"You're probably wondering what to do next?" Tick asked her.

"Yes," she replied, although she already knew what she wanted to do next; run off and shake the cherry trees to see if any fruit really dropped like it did in the commercial, and then hop in the ocean for a swim.

"There's an orientation meeting you should attend," Tock said.

Before Alana had a chance to get her bearings, a hamster dressed in a hot pink striped dress raced over to her.

"I'm Happy! I'm new here, too! We have to move quick or we will miss the orientation! It's so great to meet you." Happy spoke fast and rushed ahead of Alana before she had a chance to answer or introduce herself. Alana wondered if she'd like her new neighbors.

CHAPTER 2

ARRIVALS

Alana tried to catch her breath as she trailed behind Happy. In the distance, she could make out a green tent with a small crowd standing in front of it. By the time Alana reached the tent, she had finally caught her breath. Happy appeared to have boundless energy.

"This is the most exciting thing that has ever happened to me," Happy blurted. "I can't wait to take long runs around the island. I love being active. This looks like the best place to run because there aren't any hills. I don't like running uphill because it slows me down."

While Happy spoke, Alana surveyed the area. She saw a river a few feet from the tent and also noticed a chicken, dressed in a blue t-shirt and shorts, who appeared to be napping. She wanted to introduce herself to the chicken but didn't want to wake him. She assumed the chicken had traveled a long distance and was quite tired.

Tick and Tock stood in front of the tent labeled *Resident Life* and asked everyone to be quiet because the orientation was about to begin. Just then, a portlier racoon dressed in a Hawaiian shirt pulled back the tent's fabric door and stepped outside to stand beside Tick and Tock.

"I'm Wayne," the large raccoon announced, "and I'm the director of the island. If you have any issues, please let me know. I will also help you get settled on the island. I'm sure you have a lot of questions, but first I want to make sure that everyone is here."

Wayne pulled out a piece of paper with a list of names and called out, "Happy."

"Yes," Happy replied, "I'm here and I must say that I am so excited for this adventure. Thank you for letting me take part in this. This is going to be the best experience in my life. I can't wait to get started. Can I have my tent now?"

"I'm sorry Happy, but you must wait until the orientation is over." Wayne calmly looked down at the list and proceeded to read the next name.

"Carl."

There was no response.

"Carl," Wayne called out for a second time.

Again, there was no response.

"CARL!" Wayne raised his voice.

The chicken woke up. "Did somebody call my name?"

"Are you Carl?" Wayne asked.

"Yes, I am," he replied and drifted back to sleep.

"Carl, it's good to have you here. Can you stay awake for the orientation? This is important and I don't want you to miss out on any vital information."

"Yes, sir." Carl said with a yawn.

Wayne went back to his sheet. "Alana," he read the final name.

"Yes, I'm here," Alana's voice cracked when she spoke.

"Great, then it appears everyone is here. I think everyone met my two assistants, Tick and Tock."

Happy and Alana nodded, but Carl seemed to be back asleep.

Wayne continued, "Today is the first day on the island. I am going to provide everyone with tents. I want you to find a spot to place your tent and once you've done that, let's meet back here so we can continue."

Tick and Tock handed out the tents. Alana was shocked at how heavy the tent was. She struggled to carry it. She wanted to find the perfect spot for the tent, but carrying it was so burdensome that she wasn't able to explore the island properly. She left the tent by a cherry tree and went off to explore, unburdened by any belongings.

The first place Alana stopped was the waterfall. She stood by the majestic waterfall and felt the breeze from the water and listened to the soothing sound. She tried to imagine living by such an inspiring sight when Carl walked over to her.

"Have you placed your tent anywhere yet?" He spoke very slowly, as if each word was a struggle.

"No, I was thinking about placing it here, but I think being beside the waterfall would be a bit much. It's nice to visit here, but I'd rather be a bit more inland. I think I want to place my tent between two trees."

Carl yawned. "That seems like a good idea. Do you mind if I ask you to place my tent somewhere? I don't like making decisions. They take up so much energy."

Alana didn't know what to say. She loved making decisions and doing new things, but she didn't want to judge her new friend. She believed first impressions were often inaccurate and Alana wanted to give her new neighbor a chance. Also, she was glad Carl wasn't as hyper as Happy. She wasn't sure she could handle two energetic neighbors.

"I'm not sure I should be the one to decide where you place your tent. I mean, I don't even know you. I don't know what you like. Do you like to be by the water? Or in the shade?"

Carl sat down on the ground. "I like anything. I'm not picky. Just place my tent anywhere and I'll be happy."

Alana hoped what he was saying was true. In the past, she had done favors for people and they had criticized the way she completed their requests. She remembered when her friend Harriet was absent from school, and she asked Alana to copy an assignment for her. When she walked to Harriet's house and delivered it, Harriet was mad at Alana because she didn't write neatly enough and Harriet had to read the assignment twice.

Alana was worried that she'd place Carl's tent in a spot that he disliked, but he'd just be too lazy to complain. She tried to figure out what Carl would like by asking him questions, but he didn't seem interested in answering them.

Alana decided to delay. "I have to explore the island. I haven't even figured out where to put my tent, so I have to look around first."

"That's fine," said Carl. "I'll just wait here. Let me know where you place my tent, okay?"

Alana walked around the island. She was annoyed that she had the pressure of placing Carl's tent somewhere on the island, but she tried not to let that bother her. She walked over to the shore, but she didn't want to place her tent on the beach. She chose a spot in the center of the island, just a short walk to the Resident Life tent. Her tent was in between two cherry trees. Alana shook the trees and cherries landed in the weeds next to the tree, just as she hoped they would. She placed the cherries in her pocket and then picked up the weeds. She wanted the area surrounding her tent to be immaculate.

Now she had to place Carl's tent. She walked around the island and found a shady spot to set up Carl's tent. He was on the other side of the Resident Life tent, which meant he still lived close to her, but he wasn't too close. As she walked back to Carl to tell him where she placed his tent, Happy called out to her.

"Yoo-hoo! Red-headed girl!" Happy called out. "I don't know your name."

"It's Alana." She stopped short and sweat started to form on her brow when she saw the spot Happy had chosen for her tent. Happy's tent was right next to Alana's.

"We're going to be neighbors, Alana!" Happy exclaimed, "and I'm so excited for it. I think we're not only going to be neighbors, but best friends, don't you?"

Alana smiled. She didn't know what to say, but it didn't matter because Happy announced that she was off on her daily jog. She needed to get it in before she returned to the orientation. Apparently, she needed to do a lot of cardio, and Alana was relieved that Happy didn't wait around for a response to the friend question.

On the walk to meet Carl, Alana saw a balloon flying through the sky with a present attached to it. The wind made the present fly quickly through the air, Alana reached out to grasp it, but she couldn't grab the string. There had to be an easier way to get the balloon down. Alana made a mental note to ask this question when they returned to the orientation.

"Carl," Alana called out as she saw the chicken resting against the tree.

He woke up. "Did you find a great spot for my tent?"

"I hope so."

"Great," Carl said and followed her, but he walked so slowly that she had to stop every few minutes to let him catch up. When they reached his tent, he marveled at the spot. "You did such a great job picking out a place for my tent. I just love it. You're a good friend. I'm lucky to have you for a neighbor."

Alana was pleased she had chosen a spot that Carl liked. He walked inside his tent and remarked at how spacious it was.

"I think I want to take a nap," he announced.

"We have to get back to orientation," she reminded him, "and we don't even have beds yet."

"True," he said laconically.

Tick and Tock made an announcement on a loud-speaker which was heard across the island. "Two more minutes until orientation begins. Please be prompt."

Carl and Alana walked back to the Resident Life tent; Alana wasn't surprised that Happy was already there.

"I just jogged the fastest I ever have before," Happy told Alana.

"Great job!" Alana commended her.

Alana was surprised to hear Happy reply, "I know."

CHAPTER 3

BONFIRES AND NEW FRIENDS

Wayne invited everyone to the shore to watch the sun set. While they walked, Wayne pointed out the different plants, trees, and rocks on the island.

He paused by a rock and gestured for the others to stop. He handed Alana a shovel and instructed her to crack the rock open with it. The shovel was surprisingly cold as she grabbed it from Wayne's hands. Summoning all of her strength, she slammed the shovel into the rock, and watched as a small bag appeared amidst the rubble.

"Pick it up," Wayne said.

"What is it?" Alana asked as she handed the shovel back to Wayne and reached for the bag.

"Open it."

Alana untied the string and looked inside the bag. It was filled with brightly colored gold bells. "Bells?"

"Bells are a form of currency on this island. You can use them to pay for things. For instance, you might not want to live in a tent forever, so you can pay and get a real wooden house by using bells. You can also pay with miles." Wayne explained how the payment system worked in more detail.

At home, Alana got five dollars a week for allowance and she saved it to buy video games. In order to get her allowance, Alana had to make sure her room was clean and that her bookbag was always packed the night before school. On this new island, she could collect bells or miles to pay for everything and earning the bells seemed like a lot more fun than packing her books into her musty blue bookbag.

The sun lowered over the clear blue water, and you could see fish swimming beneath the surface. The wind grew stronger and Alana took a deep breath, filling her lungs with the clean salty ocean air.

"Isn't this beach just beautiful?" Happy said. "I jogged past this beach earlier. I can't wait to swim around the island. I bet I could swim around the entire island in five minutes. I am a very fast swimmer. What do you think, Alana? Do you think I can do it?"

"I don't know. I hope you can. It's nice to have a challenge."

Wayne looked over at Alana and Happy and said, "It's great that you're getting along so well. Alana, you seem to have a knack for getting along with people. I think you should be the island manager."

"The island manager?" Alana questioned, "what does that mean?"

"It means that you get to name the island, and you

also get to help in shaping how it looks. You can plant flowers around the island and help your neighbors decorate their houses by placing hammocks, fences, and other items around their homes."

"That sounds like a fun job, Alana. You should definitely do it." Happy jumped while she spoke.

Alana had never been in charge of anything before. Well, she was once in charge of taking care of the class hamster in third grade. She had to note when the hamster was fed and let the teacher know when they were running low on hamster supplies. Her teacher commended her on doing a good job and gave her a certificate at the end of the school year. Alana thought about Puddles the Hamster and how he was so much quieter than Happy. Puddles slept most of the day and occasionally rode on its wheel. She couldn't imagine Happy adjusting to that lifestyle.

"Yes, I'll do it," Alana announced, and she was surprised when she received a round of applause from Tick, Tock, Wayne, Happy, and even Carl who had just woken up for this monumental moment.

"Please tell us the name for this new island," Wayne requested.

Alana thought about all the names she had listed the night before. As the sun set and darkness filled the peaceful island, she couldn't believe that only twenty-four hours ago, she was in her bed. She thought about Furry and her decision to name an island after him. She announced, "Furtopia. I will name this island Furtopia."

"What a splendid name," said Wayne. "I couldn't have thought of a better name myself."

"I love it," said Happy. "You are so smart!"

Carl remarked, "As one of the furless creatures on the island, I feel a bit left out, but I guess Furtopia is okay. It makes sense."

Alana reminded Carl that she was also furless, and then added, "I'm glad you're okay with the name."

"I'm glad I didn't have to make the name up myself. That would take too much energy." Carl yawned as he said, "Isn't it time to go to bed. The sun has set, right?"

"Yes, it has," says Wayne, "but it would be nice to get to know everyone a bit better. I was thinking of making a bonfire. Of course, we can't stay up too late. Tomorrow is a big day because you all have to start developing this deserted island."

"I thought Alana was the one chosen to develop the island," said Carl. "Doesn't that mean I can sleep in and just spend my days relaxing?"

"You have to help Alana. This is a big job and she can't do it alone," instructed Wayne.

"I will help. I am a very good helper. I work very fast and I know that Alana will enjoy my help because I always do a good job." Happy went on to list and explain all the amazing jobs she had done in the past.

Alana was concerned about working alongside Happy and Carl. Happy was too energetic and Carl was quite the opposite. She wanted to be alone and think, so she walked away from the bonfire Wayne had just made with Tick and Tock and strolled along the shore. She looked out at the ocean, but it was too dark to see very far. She dipped her foot in the ocean and felt a sharp stinging sensation in her foot and cried out in pain. Happy rushed to her side, "Are you okay? What happened?"

"I don't know," Alana cried. "my foot hurts."

"Let me take a look at it," Happy carefully inspected Alana's foot, and then placed it down. She walked toward the shore and picked up a cracked shell. "You stepped on a shell and it cut your foot. It will be okay. Why don't you come sit by the bonfire with me? We can relax and have some juice. I'm sure the pain will go away quickly."

Happy held Alana's hand and led her back to the bonfire. Alana was moved by Happy's kind heart and this proved her belief that first impressions were often wrong.

Happy cleared a spot for Alana, and they felt the warmth from the bonfire. Wayne placed a tape deck on the shore and announced, "A party isn't complete without some music." He pressed play and Alana was immediately drawn into the ballad booming from the small tape deck. The singer seemed to transport Alana. She was so enthralled by his music that she forgot her foot hurt at all.

"Who is this singer? His voice is soothing and soulful. I wish I could hear him play in person," exclaimed Alana.

"I love him too," said Happy, "He's my favorite. His name is J. J. Swooner."

Wayne said, "If Furtopia wins the Prettiest Island Award, the prize is a free J. J. Swooner concert."

"Are you serious?" exclaimed Alana. "What do we have to do to win?"

Wayne said, "It's quite simple really. You just have to work hard and make the island beautiful, and the judges will make their decision."

"We're going to win and J. J. Swooner will play right here on the beach. I know if we work together, we can make it happen," said Happy.

Alana agreed.

CHAPTER 4

GOALS

Alana was used to sleeping in her bed with her thick floral comforter and soft pillows. She worried she'd have a difficult time sleeping on a hard cot surrounded by flimsy fabric tent walls, but, surprisingly, she adjusted to tent life quite easily. When she woke up, she rushed out of her tent and began to pick up all the weeds she could find on the island. Wayne had mentioned there was only a week to get ready for the contest, and she needed to make the island as beautiful as possible. As she pulled the weeds from the verdant landscape, Alana hummed the J.J Swooner song she had heard last night. The song was about a person who wanted to travel the open road and live a life of adventure, and Alana felt these lyrics personally spoke to her. She wanted to be an adventurer for as long as she could remember, and here J.J Swooner was penning songs about others who felt the same way.

There was something satisfying about weeding because it was an easy way to make a garden look cleaner and prettier. The bad part about weeding was the amount of weeds Alana had to pick. She spent at least an hour pulling weeds from Furtopia, and there were still so many weeds left to pull. Just then, while tidying the area near a cherry tree, she heard a familiar voice. It was humming along to a J. J. Swooner song.

"Good morning, Alana! How are you on this bright morning? I've already run the length of the island three times! Did you know there's a gorgeous waterfall on the island? I just wanted to sit by it all day, but I had to keep running. I need to get my miles in, you know. It's very important to stay active. Did you do any cardio this morning?"

"Good morning, Happy," Alana said without looking up. She wanted to make sure she had gotten every pesky weed growing near the cherry tree. "I have been pulling weeds. Wayne said that getting rid of the weeds would make the island prettier, and I want to win that contest because I'd love to host a J.J. Swooner concert here."

"J. J. Swooner is the best. I was humming his songs during my run. I agree, having J. J. Swooner visit would be totally awesome. How can I help you?"

"You can help by picking weeds," Alana said. "I want to meet with Wayne to get a list of everything we need to do to get the island ready for the contest. I don't want to forget anything."

"I like your energy!" Happy said as she raced off to search for weeds.

Because she stopped to pick every weed on the way, it took Alana a long time to reach the Resident Life tent where Wayne, Tick, and Tock were staying. When she finally reached the tent, she saw the three raccoons huddled together and talking in quiet voices. Wayne noticed Alana approaching and waved.

"Alana, good to see you. I was just chatting with my co-workers about the great weeding job you've done. I must say that you are a very motivated person, and I'm sure you'll be rewarded. However, this job is meant for more than one person. There is no way you can get this island in shape on your own."

"Happy is helping me weed," Alana explained.

"That's great, but you'll need more than two people to get it done efficiently."

"I will recruit Carl. Perhaps he's more energetic today because he had a good night's rest," said Alana, "I'm fairly confident I can get everyone on the island to get onboard and we will be able to win the contest."

"I like your enthusiasm. It should get you far, but will it get you far enough?" Wayne asked.

Alana assumed that was a rhetorical question. She also wondered if he was correct. Would she be able to get Carl onboard to help beautify Furtopia? She wondered if she could get other animals to join the island, because she knew that you get a lot more done with a larger group.

"Before you get back to your weeding, I want to teach you something that might help you make the island prettier," Wayne said as he opened the door to the tent and invited Alana into the Resident Services. There was a large wooden table in the corner of the tent. He explained, "This is a crafting table. Since we're on a deserted island, we have to be resourceful and create a lot of things from scratch."

"I love crafting," exclaimed Alana. She stopped herself from listing the many crafting projects she had done, from making bracelets for her friends and family to sewing a pillow that her parents displayed on their bed. She was also learning to knit. Alana didn't tell Wayne about these skills because she didn't want to gloat. She also wasn't sure anything she had learned in the real world translated to this universe. Alana had never used a crafting table before.

The table was covered with tree branches and Wayne picked one up. "I am going to teach you how to make a fishing rod."

Alana watched as he pieced together the branches to create a rod. He showed her the rod he made and said, "Now it's your turn. You need to make your own rod."

She picked up a branch and tried to recall the recipe he had just shown her. She was pleased when she successfully completed the rod—even Tick and Tock broke out in applause.

"I guess I did it correctly," she remarked with a smile.

"Yes, but there are many other items you'll need to craft," Wayne said, "and some are a bit more complicated." Wayne pulled out a smartphone from his pocket. Alana's parents used those all the time. They were always answering messages or looking things up on their phones. She wasn't allowed to have a smartphone because her mom said she was too young. She couldn't wait until she had her own, so she was thrilled when Wayne handed her the phone.

"I think you should have this phone. It will come in handy when you're on the island. The phone contains many DIY recipes for essential items. Don't lose the phone and be sure to take good care of it," Wayne said.

"I will!" Alana wanted to run back to the tent and spend the day studying the phone. She wondered what else she could do with it. However, she knew that she had to stay focused if she wanted to win the contest. The phone was meant to be an aid, not a distraction.

"Great, but before you go back to your weeding, I'd like you to try to catch a fish. Can you see how many you can catch with your new rod and then meet me back here?"

Alana nodded and raced toward the shore. As she made her way to the water, she spotted Carl lying in front of his tent next to the pieces of a cot.

"Carl," Alana said, "are you okay?"

"Shhh! I don't want to be bothered. Can't you see I'm sleeping?" Carl didn't open his eyes.

"Carl, it's way past morning and I need your help. I wish you would wake up," pleaded Alana.

"Shh! Please be quiet. It's very early."

"But it isn't," Alana rationalized, "and you need to get up and help us. Happy has been weeding all morning and so have I. You need to help us or we won't win the contest."

Carl opened his eyes, "I'm not a fan of contests."

Alana looked down at his unassembled cot and said, "It looks like you're not a fan of cots either."

Carl stood up, "I didn't feel like setting it up. It's just so much work. I found sleeping on the floor to be much easier."

Alana knew they couldn't win the contest if residents left pieces of cots in front of their tents, so she picked up Carl's cot and placed it inside the tent. He followed her into the tent and thanked her for being a good friend. Once the cot was made, he crawled onto it and wished her a good night.

"It's the afternoon," Alana said with a sigh.

CHAPTER 5

TEACH A MAN TO FISH

Alana stood on the beach and cast the rod into the ocean. She felt a pull and quickly reeled the line in, only to find a boot hanging from the hook.

"Seriously?" she said aloud and cast her line again. Alana felt a tug on the line and hoped it wasn't another boot. Luckily, this time she caught a sea bass and put it in her pocket. She cast her reel one more time and caught a flounder. As she placed the flounder in her pocket, Alana noticed a bottle wash up on shore. She picked up the glass bottle and inspected it. There was a note inside and she opened the bottle and pulled out the dry piece of paper.

Dear Stranger,
I made a few errors when I first started to craft, but I actually wound up making something useful. I am giving you the recipe I accidentally crafted. It's for a pear chair.

You'll need 3 pears and 4 pieces of wood. I love
this chair because it's both tasty and comfy.
                                        Your Friend,
                            Stranger from another village

Alana saved the note, but she didn't have any pears
and she wasn't sure how to plant any pear trees. There
was so much she didn't know, and she wanted to learn
everything as quickly as possible. Surely having a large
variety of fruit trees would make Furtopia the prettiest
island. She had to ask Wayne how one obtains seeds for
the trees.

With pockets full of fresh fish, Alana sprinted
toward the Resident Services tent ready to ask Wayne a
list of questions, but seconds after leaving the beach she
was stopped by Happy.

"I just did twenty jumping jacks and then ran
around the island three times," Happy announced.

"Wow," said Alana, "I'm impressed. Were you able
to pick up any weeds?"

"Yes, a few. I have to admit, I found picking weeds
to be slightly tedious. After a few minutes, I had the
urge to run, so I did."

"But we need to clean up the island. I can't pick all
the weeds on my own. If we don't get the island ready,
we won't win the contest. I thought you were a fan of J.J
Swooner? Don't you want him to play a concert here?"

"You know I do! It's not my fault that you asked me
to do the most boring activity ever. Can you help me
find something more interesting to do?"

While they spoke, Alana noticed another balloon with a present attached to it. The balloon floated over the sea and toward them. Alana jumped as high as she could, but she still couldn't reach it. Happy pulled a slingshot out from her pocket and aimed at the balloon. With one shot she popped the balloon and the present fell to the ground. Happy picked up the present and handed it to Alana.

"You can have this present. I feel bad that I didn't pick weeds," said Happy.

"You don't have to give me the present."

"I want to." Happy insisted that Alana open it.

Alana opened the present and discovered so many bells she couldn't count them.

"Oh my!" said Happy, "look at all those bells. I'm such a nice friend to let you have such a fantastic gift. You're a lucky person, Alana."

Alana guessed that there were thousands of glistening bells, which meant she'd be able to buy items and supplies to beautify the island, but she didn't think it was fair to keep them all. To make the choice even clearer, Happy was leaning over Alana, remarking on how lucky she was to have gotten such a rare and lavish present.

"I can't take all of these bells. Let's split them," Alana suggested.

"No, I think we should use them to help build Furtopia. Think of all the things we could do with this money," Happy said. "We have to tell Wayne. I know that Tick and Tock have a shop and they sell all sorts of items we will need to make Furtopia the prettiest island."

"What a great idea," said Alana.

Happy and Alana raced toward the Resident Life tent, but Alana lost Happy on the way. She called out Happy's name, but she was nowhere to be found.

A deep voice called out to Alana, "Did you catch a lot of fish?" Wayne was standing in front of the tent.

"I caught a few, but something incredible happened. I spotted a balloon in the sky and Happy used a slingshot to knock it down. There was a present attached which contained thousands of bells. There were so many I couldn't keep count."

"Congratulations," Tick said as he emerged from the tent with Tock.

"That is a very rare find," said Tock.

"You can give up the tent life and buy a house. I can show you a few different homes that would fit on your property. You can also buy homes for Happy and Carl," suggested Wayne.

Alana liked the idea of repaying Happy by gifting her a house, but she didn't think Carl deserved a house. He hadn't helped her one bit. In fact, he was so lazy he couldn't be bothered to place his cot inside his tent. Despite this, Alana knew she had to buy Carl a new home because Furtopia would look better if every resident had a nice, new, wooden house.

She picked up three small wooden homes that took the place of the tents. Alana walked over to Carl's new house to see what he thought, but he wasn't at home.

She searched the island and found Carl lying on the beach napping.

"Carl!" she yelled. Alana was annoyed and didn't care if she woke Carl from one of his precious naps, "Get up!"

"I wasn't sleeping. I was just soaking in the rays. You know you can never get enough vitamin D."

"I wanted you to know that I bought you a house. If you want, we could walk over and see it. Maybe I can build a fence for you and we can build a garden together."

"After I finish working on my tan, okay?" Carl said as he turned over and sunned his back.

CHAPTER 6

FOR THE BIRDS

Wayne invited Alana to use the crafting table and asked her how her day was going. Alana wanted to complain about her neighbor Carl. She wanted to tell Wayne that he slept all day and wasn't helpful at all, but she stopped herself. She wasn't a tattle and she also wanted to figure out how to handle Carl on her own. Wayne had given her the position of island manager and she wanted to show off her managerial skills. Her mom was a manager in her office and she often talked about issues with her co-workers at dinner. Alana's dad would offer advice, but Alana and her sister found these conversations utterly boring and never paid attention. Alana wished she had listened more. She did recall once when her mom was having a tough time with an employee who never finished his work on time. Her father said she should compliment him on what he did well, and maybe that would help. Alana decided she would use that approach the next time she saw Carl.

"What should I craft next?" asked Alana.

"I think a net would be nice," said Tick. "Then you can catch butterflies and other insects."

"Speaking of catching things, can I see the fish you caught?" asked Wayne.

Alana pulled out the bass and flounder from her pocket. "I also got a boot, but I don't think you want that."

Wayne chuckled and took the fish from Alana to inspect them. "Can I keep these fish? I have a friend who has a better understanding of marine life who can tell us the value of each fish."

"No problem," Alana said as her stomach grumbled. She realized that she was so excited about exploring and getting the island ready for the contest that she had forgotten to eat dinner. Alana had hoped she could cook the fish for dinner, but now she had given them away to Wayne. The lack of nourishment also made her tired. She stopped focusing on what Wayne was saying and started to think about cakes, cookies, and all the snacks she missed from home.

Alana remembered that she had picked some cherries earlier that morning. She pulled one out of her pocket and ate it while Wayne spoke. She hoped she didn't seem rude. Within seconds of eating the cherry, she felt incredibly energetic. She wondered if this was what Happy felt like all the time because she had enough energy to run around the island and also pick every weed that was sprouting on the island. Suddenly, she had an idea. She sprinted from the Resident Life tent to Carl's house. Carl was sitting outside his new wooden home.

"Do you like the new house?" asked Alana,

"It's okay. I didn't bother going in. I just want to soak in a few more rays out here." Carl's voice was weak, and she could barely make out the words he spoke.

"I have a present for you."

"You bought me a house. Don't you think you've given me enough presents for today?"

Alana smiled. "You did such a great job working on your tan, you deserve another present."

Carl perked up. "Do I really look tan?"

"Yes, you look tan and healthy."

"Wow! I never seem to accomplish anything, so this might be a first."

"I think you're just lacking energy and I think you need to eat." Alana pulled a cherry from her pocket and handed it to Carl.

"Eating takes up so much energy," he complained.

"Once you eat the cherry, you'll have energy. Then you can work on your tan while you help me pull the rest of the weeds from the island."

Carl reluctantly put the cherry in his mouth and took a bite. It didn't take long for Carl to stand up and attempt to fly. He appeared shocked and remarked, "Wow, I didn't know I could do that."

"Fly?" she questioned, "Why do you think you have wings?"

"I guess," Carl added, "but chickens aren't known for flying very far, so I never bothered to learn how to fly."

Alana spotted a patch of weeds by Carl's house. She reached over to pick up some weeds and was thrilled when Carl joined her.

"Now you can work on your tan and help weed."

"True, true," Carl said as he picked weeds alongside Alana.

Alana was happy that she was able to get Carl to help— and she didn't even need to ask Wayne to help her. She also enjoyed working alongside Carl. They were able to clear all the weeds on his side of the island. They made their way across the island, passing the Resident Life tent, when Wayne walked out of the tent with a large owl and called Alana over.

"Alana, I want you to meet my friend Feathers." He introduced Alana to the owl. "He is the marine life expert and he wanted to see if you could catch more fish. He wants to open a museum on the island and he thinks they should be on display there."

Alana had been to a museum on a school trip. She remembered the teacher constantly reminding everyone to keep their voices down and to not touch anything. The teacher explained that museums only contained important items and that some were invaluable. Alana couldn't believe something she had caught was going to be on display in a museum. This was a dream come true. She also assumed that having a museum on the island would make it more appealing and it might help their chances of winning the contest.

"Pleased to meet you, Feathers," Alana said. "This is my friend, Carl." She pointed at Carl, who was resting his head against the Resident Life tent and appeared to be asleep.

"This is a very peaceful island," Feathers remarked.

Alana giggled and thanked Feathers.

"I find the marine life surrounding this island to be fascinating and I can't wait to see what other fish you'll find."

Alana noticed a stack of wood next to the Resident Life tent and asked, "Is that the wood you're using to build the museum?"

"No," Wayne said, "Tick and Tock are building a store. Now that the island is developed, we should have a store. I'm also upgrading from a tent to an actual Resident Life building."

"I'm excited to go shopping. I was going to use my phone to do DIY recipes, but I'd also like the option of buying something that's already made," Alana said enthusiastically and then walked over to Carl and gently woke him up.

"What? Where are we?" Carl awoke confused.

"We were just about to finish weeding the island."

"That's right, and I also get to work on my tan," he said as he walked alongside Alana.

She smiled, hoping that she had finally made a breakthrough with Carl.

CHAPTER 7

ALL WORK AND NO PLAY

The next morning Alana woke up early. The day before, she had weeded the entire island with Carl and was hoping that Happy and Carl would help her plant flowers around the island and work on crafting furniture for their homes. Wayne told her the store was having its grand opening that morning and she wanted to be the first customer. As she sprinted to the store, Happy ran past her.

"Alana!" Happy called out, "Are you doing cardio? If so, I'd love to jog with you. I always love jogging with a friend."

"No," Alana explained, "I'm not running for fun, I'm heading to the new store that's opening on the island."

"A store! I love shopping!"

Alana said, "Do you want to go with me?"

"I can't. I have to finish my morning jog. I can go later today. Would you wait for me?"

"I have to go now," said Alana. "I want to buy items

to work on the island. We only have a few more days left, and I don't want to lose the contest."

"I think a nice morning jog might clear your head and make you work more efficiently."

"I don't have time for leisurely activities. I want Furtopia to be the prettiest island." Alana didn't understand why Happy and Carl weren't as focused as she was. Didn't they care about winning? She wished Happy well and sprinted off to the new store.

Tick and Tock stood by the store's entrance. "Welcome," Tick greeted her. "You're our first customer."

"Wow!" she said as she raced into the store, a rustic wooden shed, and perused the shop's inventory. Alana spotted a slingshot on the counter. She picked it up and hoped she had enough bells to purchase it. Alana needed the slingshot to shoot down the balloons that flew through the sky.

"I'd like to buy this," Alana said.

Luckily, she had enough bells to pay for the slingshot, but she was almost out of bells after purchasing those houses.

"Tick," Alana asked, "How do I earn more bells?"

"You can sell items to the shop."

"Fish, turnips . . ." Tick listed off many items that were valuable enough to sell in the shop. When he was done speaking, Feathers walked into the store.

"Hi Feathers," Alana said. She wanted to ask him if she could have the fish back so she could sell them to Tick, but she had already promised them to the museum.

"It appears that you get up early," he told Alana. "As they say, the early bird gets the worm. Speaking of getting things, can you get me some fossils? I don't want to spend my day constructing a museum if I don't have anything to display on the walls."

"Yes," Alana replied, but she wasn't sure where she'd find a fossil. Maybe she'd find one while planting flowers across the island. She wished Feathers well and left the shop ready to get started on her day's work. Alana had a list of things she must accomplish by the end of the day, and now she added finding fossils to the list, but there was no way she could do everything herself. She was racing to Carl's house when she felt a rain drop on her head. At first, she thought it was the wind blowing water from the shore, but soon the sky grew very dark and the rain pooled on the grass and her shoes were covered in mud.

By the time she reached Carl's door, she was drenched. She knocked, and he hollered out, "Go away! I'm sleeping!"

"We have to get to work," Alana told him, although she knew working in the rain was going to be a hard sell, because Carl didn't even want to work on sunny days.

"Come by later," he whined, "I need more sleep. And besides, it's raining."

"When should I come by?"

"I don't know. When the rain stops. I just want to be left alone. Can you take a hint?"

Alana left feeling hurt and disappointed. Carl wasn't helpful and she didn't think she could plant flowers. She wouldn't be able to cross anything off her list and that wasn't acceptable to her. As she walked toward her house, she spotted Happy doing jumping jacks underneath a large cherry tree. The leaves of the cherry tree covered Happy and kept her dry.

"You look sad," she remarked to Alana.

"I am and I'm also frustrated," she said. "I just wanted to get the island ready for the concert and Carl won't help and you always seem to be too busy. I just can't do it alone. I don't find it fair that you can spend the day doing whatever you please and Carl gets to sleep all day, and I'm the one doing all the work all the time. I need help. I don't want to be the only one working on the island and donating items to the museum. I need a team."

"That's what you want." Happy stopped her exercise routine and said, "But that's not what everyone wants. You never ask us what we want to do, you just tell us what we should do."

Alana's eyes filled with tears. It never occurred to her that she was dictating orders to Happy and Carl. She thought they wanted to have J. J. Swooner play a concert on the island and that it mattered to them to live on the prettiest island. She didn't understand why anybody wouldn't want to achieve these goals.

"I'm sorry. I didn't realize you guys felt that way. I'm glad you told me," Alana said as she ran to her house before Happy could see that she was crying.

She wanted to run away. She raced into her home, but there was nothing to distract her there. Her home was barren with only a bed. Alana splashed through the puddles as she raced toward the shore. She wanted to swim away from the island. When she reached the beach, the sun came out and she pulled her fishing rod out and cast it into the sea. Within minutes, Alana had caught four sea bass. She wondered if the rain had any impact on the unusually favorable fishing conditions. Alana placed the fish in her pocket when she saw another bottle wash up on the shore. She picked it up and opened the cap. The letter read,

> Dear New Friend,
>   On my island, we have lush orange trees and we spend our days relaxing and feasting on this fruit. We keep track of time with this orange clock. Here's a recipe for it. Hope to meet you one day.
>
>   Signed,
>   Your New Friend

Alana tried to picture this island and wondered if it was prettier than Furtopia. She thought about what Happy said. Maybe she was too focused on making Furtopia pretty. Maybe she could travel to another island and get away. She didn't know if this was possible, but she was going to see Wayne and ask him. As she raced to the store, she spotted a purple butterfly in the distance, and she pulled out her net and chased it until she caught it in her net. She wondered if she could sell the butterfly to Tick and Tock, and if she could use that to get a ticket off the island.

CHAPTER 8

GREAT ESCAPES

Wayne stood outside the new store. "This is a nice place, right?"

Alana nodded. "I bought a slingshot there this morning."

"You were our first customer. We couldn't have opened this shop without you. You have done so much for this island. You generously bought homes for all the residents and you've donated fish to Feather's museum. In fact, he told me you were out collecting more items for the museum."

Alana thought about the butterfly and the fish she had in her pocket. She wanted to sell them, but she did promise Feathers she would donate items to be displayed on the museum. She also wanted to tell Wayne that nobody on the island liked her and she wanted to run away.

"I'm so glad you moved here and that I made you manager," said Wayne.

"About that," said Alana.

"Is everything okay?" asked Wayne.

She decided to keep the issues brewing on the island to herself. She didn't want to appear to be a bad manager, so instead she said, "I've noticed a lot of messages in a bottle washing up on the shore, and each one has a letter from other people on different islands. I was hoping I'd be able to explore one of those islands. Is that possible?"

"Of course!" Wayne said. "There are numerous islands out there to explore. Residents around the Animal Crossing Universe send their best DIY recipes from their respective islands to help others. Because the message floats over in a bottle, tracking down the sender is near impossible, but it's still a great way to learn about new recipes. There's another thing you should know. A visit to another island can help you make this island prettier."

Alana didn't understand how that might be the case. How could traveling to another island help this one? She was worried that leaving the island would slow down her progress, but without Happy and Carl's help, the island wasn't going to win the contest anyway.

Wayne explained, "When you visit another island, you will be able to extract resources from that island. For instance, if the island has apple trees, you can pick apples and then use the apples to populate Furtopia with apple trees. You might find many other goodies on the other island and meet a new friend."

A friend. Alana's heart raced. She wanted to meet a friend badly. Alana thought Happy could be her friend, but after their last conversation, she didn't think that was likely to happen, and she didn't even know where to begin with Carl. He wasn't trying to be anyone's friend; he just wanted to sleep and soak in the rays.

"How do I get to another island?"

Wayne told her about an excursion package, which enables Alana to travel to another undeveloped island, "You can purchase a ticket from me."

"I don't have too many bells left, but I have some fish and a butterfly I could sell."

Luckily, the items Alana had collected were worth enough to purchase a ticket.

"When can I leave?" She asked.

"As soon as today," Wayne told her. "I have a seaplane docked at the pier, so you can leave in just a few minutes."

"Wow!" Alana exclaimed. "Okay. I'm ready to go now."

Alana saw Happy jogging toward them. Carl was slowly walking behind her. She wondered if they were approaching the tent to issue a formal complaint about Alana. It was obvious they thought she was a bad manager.

"We came to check out the store," said Happy.

Alana noticed Happy didn't greet her or look her in the eye. She greeted both Happy and Carl, but neither responded to her. Alana wished she was on the seaplane off to explore an unchartered island. She wanted to be alone.

"Great," Wayne said, "Go inside the shop and Tick and Tock will be happy to help you. I'm busy at the moment, but I'll be back soon."

Happy and Carl never acknowledged Alana before they entered the shop. With every step Alana took toward the pier, she knew she was making the right decision. She had to get away from Furtopia for a bit. When she returned to Furtopia, she'd hopefully have enough new resources to keep it in the running for "prettiest island." As she climbed aboard the plane, she thought she heard Happy call out her name, but when she turned around there wasn't anybody there.

CHAPTER 9

EXPLORATIONS

The seaplane departed from the dock while Alana looked out the window. She was anxious to see an island appear in what seemed like a never-ending blue sea. This time there wasn't a film previewing what occurred on this new island, so Alana didn't know what to expect. The plane descended. From the window, Alana could only make out just a sliver of the island. The plane glided over the calm waters and came to a standstill by a dock. The strong smell of salt permeated the air as she stepped onto the new island and saw large apple trees in the distance. She waited on the dock, but Tick and Tock weren't there to greet her. There wasn't an orientation like she had when she arrived on Furtopia. She was grateful that she wouldn't be tasked with the job of island manager here and didn't have to create a new community. It was nice to simply visit a place for a brief time period. It made her feel silly to think that she already needed a vacation after just a few days on Furtopia, but then again, establishing a new island is hard work.

Alana left the comfort of the wooden pier that housed the seaplane and bravely explored the island. It was midafternoon and the sun was shining. Sweat formed on her brow. She stopped underneath an apple tree and enjoyed the cooling breeze from the ocean. Alana shook the tree and jumped out of the way to avoid having apples land on her head. The apples fell to the ground and she quickly picked them up and filled her pockets. She wished she had the chest that she kept at home. She worried that she didn't have the capacity to carry everything she needed.

The island was full of apple trees. Alana didn't know if she should try to empty every tree on the island. She paused and took a bite of the apple. It was one of the juiciest and tastiest apples she had ever eaten.

"I must take every apple I can. I bet Tick and Tock would offer me a lot of bells for these apples. I can't wait to use one of these apples to grow apple trees on Furtopia," she said aloud.

"Who are you talking to?" a voice called out.

Alana gasped. She was embarrassed but also surprised by the voice. Who could be there? She couldn't see anyone.

"Are you going to eat all the apples? Don't be greedy."

The voice was louder so Alana assumed they were getting closer.

"Plus, you'll have the worst stomachache ever. I know because I once ate three apples and I had just the most awful stomachache. I feel a duty to warn you."

"I am not eating every apple," Alana explained as she looked up and around to find out where the voice was coming from.

"Over here!" the voice laughed, and then a pig wearing a bowtie and a button-down shirt and black shorts appeared from behind an apple tree.

"Hi," Alana said, walking over to introduced herself. "I'm Alana."

"I'm Lars."

"Nice to meet you, Lars," Alana responded, smiling. She wasn't going to ask him to aid her in her search for resources so she could get J. J. Swooner to play on Furtopia; she was just going to be friendly and see what Lars wanted to do.

"Is it? You don't know me. Perhaps meeting me isn't so nice," he said laughing.

"That's a joke, right?" Alana was a little confused by Lars.

"Yes, or I mean I guess," Lars explained. "You're the first visitor here in a very long time so I'm realizing that I need to brush up on my social skills. I bet you come from a place where you have tons of friends and you guys gather on the shore and watch the sunset each night. I bet you have bonfires and help each other craft DIY projects."

"Yes," Alana lied and corrected herself. "I guess. I mean, it's complicated."

"What's complicated about having friends? I wish I had some company on this island, and now you've arrived. Perhaps you will stay here."

"I can't. I actually manage the island that I live on. It's called Furtopia."

"Wow!" Lars said. "It sounds like it's filled with a lot of furry friends."

Alana paused. She didn't know how to answer that question. She didn't want to bore him with a story about her beloved stuffed teddy bear, or the drama that was taking place on Furtopia, or the fact that Carl the chicken was annoyed that the island was called Furtopia when he head feathers instead of fur, so she just smiled and said, "Not everyone is furry, but it's a beautiful place. We only have cherry trees, so I was excited to see apple trees here. I really missed eating apples and I must say that these are the tastiest apples I've ever eaten."

"Really?" Lars shrugged. "I've had better."

"Well, I enjoyed them, so thank you for letting me take some."

"This island could be nicer. I don't think I'd ever describe this place as beautiful. You must be from a scenic island. This island is so basic. I'll give you a tour and you can see what we have. There's a pond with koi fish and a river filled with run-of-the-mill fish that you could basically find anywhere. The only cool thing we have on the island are the coconut trees that sprout on the shore. If I didn't have my daily coconut, I'd be really upset. That's the only thing this island has to offer."

"That can't be true," Alana said.

"When I'm done showing you around, you'll see that I'm correct." Lars walked Alana toward the shore. He wanted to show off the coconut tree.

Alana walked alongside Lars as he rattled off another list of reasons that his island, which had no name, was inadequate. "It's so inadequate," he explained, "that nobody bothered to name it."

"Why don't you name it?"

"Why should I bother?" he replied.

Lars reminded her a bit of Carl. Both of them didn't enjoy the simple adventure of living on an undeveloped island where you could create anything you wanted. When they reached the coconut tree he said, "This, however, isn't inadequate. It's perfection. Take a coconut and see for yourself."

Alana shook the tree and three coconuts fell on the sand. She wasn't sure if she should take all of them. She picked one up and ate it.

"Wow!" she exclaimed, "you're right, this coconut is fantastic."

"It's adequate," he said and picked up one of the coconuts and ate it.

"Do you mind if I take the other one that dropped? I'd love to bring it back to Furtopia and plant a coconut tree on our shore."

"Of course, everyone should enjoy having this tree on their island. If you'd like to shake the tree again, you can take a few more coconuts."

"Thank you." Alana shook the tree and a new batch of coconuts landed in the sand. She filled her pockets with coconuts, and then pulled out her fishing rod. "Do you mind if I fish?"

"Be my guest." Lars added, "But try not to be

disappointed with the fish you get. Remember I warned you that we only have basic fish in these waters."

Alana cast her net into the water and felt a tug and reeled in the fish, "A seabass. That's not bad."

"If that's what you like. I am a little *over* sea bass. I like more exotic fish."

Alana continued to cast her net. Each time she reeled in a seabass. She understood how Lars had grown tired of catching the same fish over and over. When Alana placed her fishing rod back in her pocket Lars said, "See? I told you it's inadequate."

Lars told her he'd show her the rest of the island. As they strolled toward a pond with koi fish, Alana pulled out her rod again. She cast the net, and pulled a rare, orange, spotted fish out and into her pocket. Lars commented, "The koi and the coconuts are the only thing worth anything on this island."

The sun was beginning to set, and Alana decided she was done exploring for today. Her pockets were filled with resources that could help Furtopia. She wanted to head back. She was exhausted from exploring, but she was also exhausted by Lar's negativity. Truthfully, he wasn't the ideal tour guide. As they walked toward the pier, Lars was humming a tune.

"Is that a J. J. Swooner song?" asked Alana.

"Yes," said Lars. "He's my favorite singer in the world. I would do anything to hear him play live."

"Do you know that if your island wins the prettiest island contest, J. J. Swooner plays a concert on the island?"

"Yes, but nobody would give this inadequate island an award unless they were truly lacking in taste or the competition was pitiful. I'd try to spruce up this island, but I can't do it alone, so I am left to spend a lifetime listening to J. J. Swooner on my old and often broken tape deck. Whenever it works, I get that small pleasure."

Alana knew how hard it was to get an island in shape on her own. She said to Lars, "If Furtopia wins the contest, you can come hear J. J. Swooner play." In the back of her mind, she felt that Furtopia winning was a longshot. She actually dreaded returning to Furtopia where she was going to have to attempt to beautify the island on her own.

"Thank you for invite. I hope you win, and I do hope I get to visit Furtopia. It sounds like a truly adequate island."

Alana hopped on the plane. When it took off, she felt a pain in her stomach. She wasn't sure if her stomach hurt because she had eaten too many apples or because she had to return to Furtopia.

CHAPTER 10

New Neighbors

It was nighttime when the plane glided on the water toward the dock. In the darkness, Alana exited the seaplane, stepped onto the dock, and yawned. She was ready to go to bed, but there was one thing she wanted to do first. With the coconut in her hand, she took a late-night stroll to the shore. Alana pulled out a shovel, dug a hole in the sand, and placed the coconut deep within the beach surface. She wanted Happy and Carl to wake up and see a coconut tree sprouting from their beach. She considered it a peace offering. Alana covered the hole in the ground with sand, using her hands. When the hole was filled in and coconut was planted properly, she walked toward her home.

As she crawled into bed, she thought about the day she spent exploring the other deserted island, and about Lars. She had spent the entire day on the island, but she never saw his home. She wondered where he lived on the island. Alana needed to get sleep because she had to wake up early to sell all the goods she had gathered from the island. She hoped Tick and Tock would buy everything from her. She also thought about Feathers. He might want some of the fish, especially the koi fish. Alana fell asleep dreaming of a museum that displayed the koi fish she had caught.

The sun shone through her window, but that wasn't what woke Alana. She had slept through many a sunrise. This morning she was jostled out of bed by a knock on the door. She rubbed her eyes, opened the door, and let out a gasp.

"A gasp! That wasn't the type of reaction I was hoping for," Lars said as he stood in her doorway.

"I am happy to see you," she explained, "I was just surprised. I didn't expect to see you on Furtopia so soon."

"The way you spoke about the island, I couldn't resist hopping on a seaplane and taking a look. The minute I arrived, I saw the luscious coconut tree and knew I was home."

"Home?" Alana questioned.

"Yes," said Lars. "I'm going to move to Furtopia. I can either live here with you or you can build me a house."

Alana didn't know how to process all this information, so she suggested they visit the store together. "I can ask Wayne, who is in charge of the island, about getting you a house."

"Perhaps I am mistaken, but I thought you were the island manager," Lars said as he stood in front of Alana's house.

As he spoke those words, Happy, who was on her morning jog, stopped and said, "Be warned: Alana takes her job as manager quite seriously."

"Isn't that a good thing?" Lars asked.

"It depends. Sometimes you can be too focused. Alana doesn't leave any time for fun activities. I've never even seen her do a bit of cardio," Happy explained.

"Not everyone finds cardio fun," Alana remarked, irritated.

Happy shook her head, and said, "Seriously? There are no words. Everyone thinks jogging is fun. So, I'm off for a jog." And with that comment Happy raced toward the beach.

Lars remarked, "She never introduced herself."

"That's Happy, and I don't think she's Happy with me at the moment. In fact, I don't think the other resident, Carl, is happy with me either. This is why I escaped to your island. I needed a break."

"It sounds like you were running away."

"Maybe I was."

"Perhaps I can help you," Lars suggested.

"How?"

"Let me get settled here first and I'll see if I could help smooth things over with the other two residents. I am known for my charming personality," Lars said. Then he remarked on how long the walk was to the store, how hot it was, and asked why the island wasn't populated with trees to provide shade.

"I am still trying to get the island in order, and I didn't have time to plant trees."

"Let's stop for a moment so you can put an apple in the ground and plant a tree," said Lars.

Alana was digging a hole in the grass when she heard someone call out to her. It was Carl. He was running toward her.

"Alana! Did you see the coconut tree that sprouted on the ocean? I think it's magical. How can something like that appear overnight?"

"I planted it," Alana explained, "and right now I'm planting an apple tree."

"I wish I could be motivated like you. You've really changed the island."

Lars said, "I'm sure you can learn to be motivated. I'm Lars and I just moved to Furtopia and I'd be glad to help you work on projects to beautify the island."

"I might take you up on that offer," Carl said with a yawn, "but right now I am going to soak in the rays and eat some coconuts."

Lars and Alana reached the store to find Wayne and Feathers standing outside.

"Alana, I'm so glad you're here," said Wayne. "We were just chatting about the museum grand opening that's scheduled for tomorrow morning, but first Feathers needs more artifacts."

"I'm stressed knowing that the museum opening may be delayed. I need more items and if I don't have them, we can't open," Feathers added.

Alana pulled out a koi fish and handed it to Feathers.

"Oh my," Feathers exclaimed, "it's been years since

I've seen a koi fish. This is indeed a rare find. What a treat. I can't wait to display this at the museum. Now we can open. But first I must ask, where did you find this beautiful fish?"

Lars responded, "She found it on the island where I used to live. I'm going to live in Furtopia now, and I'm very excited to check out your museum."

"Who are you?" Feathers asked.

"I'm Lars. I'm the newest resident on Furtopia."

"Welcome, Lars. I'm Feathers."

Wayne also introduced himself, and invited Lars into the store. "We have to build you a new home," he said. "Alana will help you build one."

Alana smiled and said, "Of course." They entered the shop to help Lars find a home, and to purchase other essentials to start his new life on Furtopia.

CHAPTER 11

TREASURE HUNT

Lars settled on a home near the museum. At his request, Alana planted cherry and apple trees in front of his house. He was pleased with the house and the trees, but he also wanted a garden with purple, pink, and yellow flowers, which Alana planted for him.

"I think we should build a fence around the garden, don't you? We should also build a pond where we can spawn some koi fish. That would make me less homesick, and we'd also make Feathers happy. He seemed to love that fish. We should do that too, shouldn't we?" Lars said as Alana built the fence,

Alana noticed that every time Lars said the word "we" he really meant her. She hoped that when Lars moved to Furtopia he would help her get the island ready for the contest. They only had a few days left, and she still hadn't completed most items from her list. She had a lot of work to do.

Lars said, "I think we need a break now. Look at how much we've done today. We placed my house and planted a garden. This means we deserve a break. Let's go to the beach."

Alana didn't have time to go to the beach, but she wondered if she took time to be with the residents and partook in leisurely activities, maybe she'd become better friends with them. Also, she felt like it was too late to win the contest. She wasn't going see J. J. Swooner live, so she should give up that dream.

As they walked to the beach, they walked past Carl's house and he was sitting in front of the house with his eyes closed.

"Carl," Alana said, "I'm sorry to wake you, but—"

Carl awoke and interrupted Alana. "I'm up! What do you want me to do? Pick more weeds?"

"No," Alana said, "I'm going to the beach with Lars and I was wondering if you'd like to join us."

"Yes," Carl said, which shocked Alana. "I'd love that. I can't get enough of those coconuts."

"Me too!" Lars exclaimed. "I'm the reason they're on this island. I told Alana to bring them here."

As the trio walked toward the beach, Alana spotted something glistening in the ground and pointed it out. "What's that?" she asked.

"That's buried treasure," Lars explained. "You should dig it up. Who knows what you'll find."

"Really? Buried treasure!" Alana pulled out her shovel and dug as fast as she could. This was a dream come true, Alana had always wished that she would stumble upon buried treasure, or at the very least a treasure map, but it hadn't happened until today. She dug and dug, but she didn't find a treasure chest. She placed her hand deep inside the hole and grabbed hold of what felt like a bone.

"You found the fossil," a voice called out. Alana turned around and found Happy standing behind her.

"How did you know?" Alana pulled the fossil out of the hole.

"I buried it. I didn't think you'd bother digging it up," Happy said.

"I've always wanted to find buried treasure," said Alana. "I bet Feathers would love this fossil. He said the museum is going to open soon, and once it does, I'm sure it could help our island win the contest. We only have a few more days."

"That's not the reason I buried the treasure. I wanted you to go on a treasure hunt and have fun."

"You planned a treasure hunt for me?" Alana asked.

"Yes," said Happy, "I thought it would be fun. Truthfully, I love planning treasure hunts. I find great hiding spots and I get to jog around the island. I get to be creative and fit in my cardio sessions."

"We were about to go to the beach, but I'd love to do your treasure hunt first," Alana explained. "Would you guys like to join me?" she asked Lars and Carl.

"Of course," said Lars. "A treasure hunt sounds like fun, and it will help me explore the rest of Furtopia."

"No," Carl said, "it sounds exhausting. Meet me at the beach when you're done."

"I'll join!" Happy said. "I promise not to give away any clues. I am so excited you're doing this."

Alana looked down at the ground for signs of buried treasure. She noticed a couple of weeds that hadn't been pulled, and she reached down to pick them when Happy said, "Alana! This isn't the time to pick weeds, it's the time to pick treasure."

Alana resisted picking weeds and sprinted across the island with Happy in search of more glistening signs of treasure.

"I knew I could get you to do some cardio with me," said Happy.

In the distance Alana spotted a circle in the ground and quickly pulled out her shovel, but before she started digging she noticed a book on the ground.

"Does this belong to any of you?" Alana asked.

"No," Happy and Lars said in unison.

"I bet it's Feathers's book. He shouldn't leave things on the ground. We'll never win the contest if we don't have a clean island."

"Alana! Stop worrying about the island. I worked really hard creating this treasure hunt and I want you to enjoy it."

Alana wondered if she could finish the entire hunt without fixating on getting the island in shape for the contest. She was annoyed at herself. She had always wished she could be on a treasure hunt, and now she almost interrupted the hunt to pick a stray weed.

"Also, I forgot to tell you," said Happy, "you only have six minutes to search for all the treasure."

With that news, Alana realized she was already losing time and she had to immerse herself in the hunt.

Within seconds she stumbled upon a star shape in the ground where she suspected there was some buried treasure. She pulled out her shovel and dug and unearthed a present. She held the gift box in her hands and inspected it. Happy walked over and undid the bow. Inside the box was a cute blue hat.

Alana put the hat on immediately and Happy remarked, "I knew that would look cute on you." It was at that moment that Alana realized Happy didn't dislike her. She was just trying to show Alana that they could do plenty of other fun things together besides creating the prettiest island.

CHAPTER 12

CLEANING IS CARING

Alana, Lars, Happy, and Carl sat at the beach and feasted on coconuts. Happy couldn't sit still for long.

"Anyone up for a swim?" she asked.

"Yes," the crowd called out in unison, and Alana was shocked to hear Carl agreed to go for a swim. Alana felt a sting in her left foot as she walked toward the water, and she cried out in pain.

"Are you okay?" Happy asked.

Alana looked at her foot. She had stepped on a glass bottle and broke the skin. Happy helped Alana clean the wound with sea water, and then she handed the bottle to Alana.

"You should open it," Happy said. "It will make you feel better."

After drying her hands on her shirt, Alana opened the bottle and read the letter inside.

To Whomever Gets This Bottle:
I love crafting musical instruments, so I'm including a DIY recipe for a bamboo drum. I hope you decide to craft it and create a concert on your island. Life is always better when you're listening to music.

Signed,
Music Lover

"Life is always better when you're listening to music. I couldn't have said it better myself," Lars said and then began humming a J. J. Swooner song.

"I'm going to make this drum," Alana said. "I think it would be nice to have a singalong on the beach. Now that we're not going to have J. J. Swooner play here, we can still make our own music."

"We don't know if our island will win or lose yet," Happy remarked.

"Let's be realistic. There's lots of work to be done, but we're on the beach. I think we'd have to put fun aside if we want to win that contest," explained Alana, "but you guys have taught me that being friends and enjoying a day at the beach is also important, and I don't want to spend my time on Furtopia being obsessed with having J. J. Swooner perform here."

Alana was surprised to hear Happy say, "Who says getting the island in shape can't be fun? If we all work together, we can have fun while we clean."

Carl said, "I will gladly help if I don't have to do too much."

Lars added, "I'm much better at coming up with ideas than I am at getting them done. I like to think of myself as more of a manager type."

Alana looked down at her foot. It was beginning to feel better, so she stood up on the beach. "I'm glad you guys want to help me, but I think I'd like to go for a swim first."

It had been a long time since Alana swam in the ocean. She usually swam in pools, but she loved swimming with the fish and exploring the marine life. Alana tasted the salty water as she swam back to shore. When she reached the shore, she pulled out a towel and took a nap on the beach underneath the coconut tree. When she awoke, she was surprised to find herself all alone.

She called out to her friends, but there was no response. Alana put her towel away and had begun searching for them when she was stopped by Feathers.

"I have one day to get everything together and I am overwhelmed with work. Can you help me?" he asked.

Although she wanted to find her friends, she saw that Feathers was frazzled. He paced as he waited for a reply. "Of course I'll help."

"Great!" Feathers exclaimed. "I will reward you with some useful tools if you help me."

"I'm not helping you because I want to be rewarded. I *want* to help."

"I know, but I think all good acts should have some reward, don't you?"

Alana didn't totally agree with that statement, but she *was* excited to get new tools. She wondered if she could use those tools to unearth treasures Feathers could display on the walls of the museum.

The museum building was majestic. It had large columns and two enormous ornate doors. It looked more impressive than the museum she had visited with her class on a school trip. Feathers opened one of the doors and led Alana into the museum. The entrance-way was grand with a large marble staircase and high ceilings with murals painted on them. Alana felt like the building itself was a work of art, and it was stunning despite being empty.

"What do you need my help with?" asked Alana.

"Can't you see? This place is barren!" Feathers voice cracked when he spoke. He walked them into a large room with floor-to-ceiling fish tanks. One of the tanks had the lone koi fish swimming in it and the other had the seabass. "We can't open a museum with two fish. Do you see how large these tanks are? We only have two fish for six big tanks."

"I can go fishing," suggested Alana.

"This isn't even the worst of it," he said as he led her to a room labeled *fossils*. The fossil exhibit was a room filled with empty walls.

"I don't even have a single fossil."

Alana recalled the fossil she had gotten during Happy's treasure hunt and pulled it from her pocket. "I have a fossil," she said. "I'd be more than happy to donate it to the museum."

"I knew you'd be a big help! This is fantastic!"

Feathers took the fossil, wiped it with a cloth and

carefully placed it on the museum's wall. "I guess one fossil is better than none, right?"

"I know this museum is going to be filled with treasures one day," said Alana.

Feathers handed Alana a gold shovel. "This should help you find more fossils."

"Thank you," Alana replied. "Do you need any more help?"

"No, I think I'm good for now."

Alana left the museum and searched for her friends. She walked to Lar's house, but he wasn't home. She was about to head to Carl's house when she saw all three of them in the distance. Happy was planting a garden, Lars was constructing a pond, and Carl was picking the few weeds that remained on the verdant green landscape. She paused for a second and stared at her friends. As she took a deep breath, inhaling the clean air that smelled faintly of flowers, she finally felt like she was home.

CHAPTER 13

BUGGING OUT

Wayne, Tick, and Tock were standing outside the store when Alana walked up.

"Alana," said Tock, "you might want to come inside. We just got in a new shipment of inventory. There's a cute crafting table you might like."

Alana had tried to craft her own table for DIY projects, but it wasn't as nice as the one she had used in the Resident Life building. If she was going to get the island in shape, she needed to buy this table.

"I can't wait to see it!" Alana raced into the store and immediately spotted the white table that was perfect for DIY projects. Next to the table was a matching white bed with a canopy, a white tape deck, and the most adorable heart-shaped wall clock. She would love to have a well-matched house with super cute furniture, but when she calculated how much it would cost her, she didn't have enough bells. She pulled some apples from her pocket, a few sea bass, and a bunch of weeds, and asked Wayne how much it was all worth.

After selling her loot, Alana still only had enough to buy the table, but she knew that she could make a bunch of items with that table that were just as cute as the ones she couldn't buy. She'd be able to decorate her apartment and the island. As she picked up the table and left the store, she noticed an acoustic guitar leaning against a wall by the exit.

"How much is that guitar?" she asked.

She didn't have enough. She considered whether she should buy the DIY table to get the guitar and make music with her friends. Alana imagined sitting on the beach as Lars played the drums and she strummed the guitar. They could sing J. J. Swooner songs all the time and wouldn't have to wait for him to play a show on the island.

Tick said, "You know, you can craft a guitar yourself."

"Thanks, I think I might," said Alana, and she left with the crafting table.

When she reached her house, she opened the door and looked for the perfect spot for the table. After placing it in the corner by the window, she imagined the other cute furniture she had seen alongside it in the room and hoped that one day she'd have enough bells to properly decorate her place.

Alana quickly got to work on crafting a long dining table, so she could invite her friends over for dinner. She opened the chest she kept beside her bed and pulled out the wood to build the table. While she crafted the table, she came up with the idea of building a swing she could place outside her door where she could hang out and chat with her friends. When the dining table was complete, she opened the chest to get more wood for the swing but there wasn't any more.

She decided to knock down a tree near her house. She grabbed her ax and headed for the decaying tree. Alana didn't like chopping down trees, but this one no longer bore fruit and it looked like it might fall down in a storm. She slammed the ax into the tree but was surprised to hear buzzing. Within seconds, Alana was surrounded by wasps. She sprinted as fast she could to get away from the insects without getting stung. When she was in the comfort of her home, she realized that Feathers might want one of the wasps to display in the museum. She pulled out her net and bravely went back outside to capture a wasp.

There were a few stray wasps flying about. Alana was able to catch one without injury. She walked the wasp over to the museum where she found Feathers outside planting a garden of red and yellow lilies.

"I have something for you," she said.

"Oh great! I knew you'd come back with something great."

Alana showed him the captured wasp in her net and Feathers jumped back.

"WHAT? GET THAT AWAY!" Feathers shouted.

"I thought you'd like the wasp. It's an insect and you don't have any in the museum."

"I don't like bugs," he announced.

"I don't want that near me," he said in a stern voice.

Alana didn't realize how much the wasp would upset Feathers. She apologized, but she forgot to put the wasp away.

"GET AWAY!" Feathers screamed as he dodged its flight path. "LEAVE!"

Alana caught the wasp and walked away from the museum. She couldn't believe how upset she had made Feathers. She felt terrible. He had just gifted her a gorgeous golden shovel and now he was banishing her from the museum.

Lars called out, "Alana, what happened? I saw Feathers yelling at you. Does he want you to leave the island?"

"I made a mistake and I upset him. I feel so bad about it, but I don't know what to do."

"What did you do?" Lars asked.

Alana told him about giving Feathers the wasp, and he remarked, "I guess he's scared of bugs or, at the very least, wasps. Have you ever been stung by a wasp? It's very painful. It happened to me and I was in pain for days. It's no fun at all. Perhaps he'd been stung in the past and didn't want it to happen again."

"I don't know, but I have to find a way to make it up to him," Alana said and walked back to her house.

On the way home, she picked up the wood she had cut down and went inside to craft the swing for outside her house. She had to distract herself, because she couldn't stop thinking about Feathers's reaction to the wasp. When the porch swing was finally complete, she placed it in front of her house and swung as she looked out at the water in the distance. As the sun set she wished Happy, Carl, or Lars would walk by and they could all watch the sunset on the new swing. She felt like she had been swinging forever when Happy jogged toward her.

"I'm so glad I caught you in time! I wanted to be able to say goodbye."

"Goodbye?" Alana was confused.

"Everyone knows you're being asked to leave." Happy had tears in her eyes as she spoke.

"I am?" she asked as the swing slowed to a stop.

CHAPTER 14

NIGHT FISHING

Alana's eyes swelled with tears. The sun had set and it was growing dark. She couldn't believe she was being kicked off Furtopia and that Happy knew about this before she did. Alana assumed Feathers complained to Wayne about the wasp incident, but she couldn't believe Wayne didn't reach out to her for an explanation. When she signed up for this adventure, she didn't think it would end this way. Alana was never kicked out of anything before. In fact, she had never been in trouble. At school she was once awarded an "Ideal Student" certificate because she had helped clean up the classroom after a messy art activity. How could she be kicked off an island? Now she'd never be able to see J. J. Swooner perform. She had so many questions, but she could only spit out the same old question, "I am?"

A firefly flew past her, and its body began to glow, briefly illuminating the night sky. The sky was dotted with stars and there was a cool sea breeze blowing through. Ironically, Alana was miserable on this perfect night.

"I'm really going to miss you," Happy said as she sat beside Alana on the swing, "I really did want to get the island ready for the concert. I'm sorry I wasn't more helpful."

"I saw you guys cleaning the island earlier today. I know you wanted to help. I'm also sorry that I was so bossy. I just really wanted to have J. J. Swooner play a concert on Furtopia, but now all I want to do is stay on the island. Do you know when I have to leave?"

Happy paused. "I don't know." She began to cry. "But I know it's soon."

Alana imagined Wayne, Tick, and Tock knocking on her front door and telling her that she had to leave the island because of what she did to Feathers. She would try to explain that she was trying to give him a donation, but they wouldn't understand. She imagined them walking her onto the seaplane in silence without being wished a good trip hone. Alana would arrive home and her parents would ask her how the adventure had been, and she wouldn't know what to say.

Alana sat in silence for so long that Happy asked her what she was thinking, but she didn't know what to say. Then she realized something: a way to solve this problem.

"I have to apologize to Feathers. I have to explain that I was trying to donate the wasp and that I wasn't trying to hurt or upset him," Alana said. "Then Wayne will understand that I didn't do anything wrong and he'll let me stay on the island."

"That sounds like a good plan," Happy said as she swung on the swing.

Alana noticed Carl approaching the house. When he reached the house, he asked Happy and Alana to make room for him on the porch swing.

"This is new. I like it. I get to move without having to do much work," he said with a yawn, and then added, "I hear you're leaving Furtopia. Sorry to hear that. Do you know who will replace you? I assume we need a new manager and I hope Wayne doesn't think I'm going to do the job. As you can imagine, I don't want that type of responsibility."

"Aren't you upset?" Happy began to cry again. "Alana is leaving us. She's going home. This is so awful."

"I'm sure they'll find a good replacement. Maybe you can be the manager, Happy," Carl said coldly.

"I don't want to be the manager. I want my friend Alana to stay on the island. I want to hear J. J. Swooner sing on our beach while I am standing beside my best friend. I don't want her to leave."

Despite being utterly heartbroken about leaving, Alana smiled. She couldn't believe Happy had referred to her as her best friend. "Thank you, Happy. I also want to stay."

"I have a great idea!" Happy exclaimed. "Let's go to the shore and go fishing at night. When you fish during the nighttime you have a good chance of finding rare fish. You can give one of those fish to Feathers and maybe he'll forgive you and then you can stay on the island."

Alana recalled how Feathers had reacted to the koi fish. He was overjoyed to receive it. She also remembered the empty tanks on display in the museum. She bet he'd be thrilled to have another fish.

The trio walked to the water and watched as Alana cast her net into the dark water. She stood on the shore waiting for a pull, but there was nothing. She looked at the water to see if she could spot any fish swimming below, but she didn't see anything.

"Are you sure fish swim on the shore at night? Maybe they're sleeping." Alana questioned.

"I don't think fish sleep," said Carl, "but then what do I know? I'm not a fish. Speaking of sleeping, I think I'm going to take a nap." Carl curled up in a ball on the sand and closed his eyes.

Happy nudged him. "You can't fall asleep now, Carl! We have to help Alana. If she doesn't catch a fish, this plan will never work, and she'll have to leave Furtopia."

Alana said, "Happy, please stop saying things like that. It makes me upset. We have to remain positive."

Carl stood up. "Okay, I'll nap later, but will you catch a fish already. I am so bored."

As Carl spoke those words, Alana felt a tug on the net. "I think I got something!" Alana exclaimed.

She reeled the line in and saw a large strange-looking fish on the line. Its head and tail were small but its body was large. The longer she looked at the fish, the more it looked like a football. Happy said, "That's a football fish. They're very rare."

Alana quickly put the fish in her pocket. "We have to show this to Feathers. I bet he will forget all about what happened this afternoon and forgive me."

"Do you think Feathers is up?" asked Carl. "Maybe we should wait until morning," he yawned, "I need to get some sleep."

"Owls are nocturnal," Alana said. She had studied nocturnal birds in school and knew that chickens like Carl weren't nocturnal and needed to sleep at night while owls were nocturnal and slept during the day.

She raced toward the museum with Happy beside her and sleepy Carl slowly trailing behind them.

CHAPTER 15

MUSEUM FINDS

Feathers was outside the museum finishing his gardening when he saw the trio approach and saw Alana pull something from her pocket.

"STOP!" he yelled. "I don't want to see the wasp again. I was finally getting over what happened earlier."

Alana explained, "I don't have a wasp with me, but I'm glad you're getting over what happened. Does this mean I get to stay on the island?"

"You were asked to leave the island? Why?" Feathers was perplexed.

Happy said, "Yes, everyone knows you told her to leave the island and now she has to go."

"I never told her that," Feathers defended himself.

Carl said, "Everyone knows you told Alana to leave the island and now we are hoping you'll be kind enough to let her stay."

Feathers was adamant that he didn't ask Alana to leave and that it was just a rumor or gossip. "I was just upset because she showed me a wasp. Despite how I love a full museum with a wide array of items on display, I guess I should have let Alana know that I am dreadfully afraid of bugs. I am scared of being stung by wasps and I'm also scared of bugs that don't sting."

As he spoke, a firefly flew near him. He screamed in terror and ran into the museum. Alana pulled out her net and caught the brightly-lit bug. She walked into the museum with Happy and Carl following her. They found Feathers shaking in the museum's entranceway.

"Is the firefly gone?"

"Yes," Alana said. "I caught it with a net."

"Then it's not gone, it's here. Can you stop assaulting me with bugs?" Feathers's teeth chattered as he spoke.

"I'm not assaulting you. I have the firefly in a safe place, and I won't take it out unless you ask me to do it," Alana's voice was calm. She put her hand in her pocket and pulled out the football fish. "I wanted to donate this fish to the museum."

"A football fish." Feathers's demeanor changed, and he appeared much calmer. "Those are exceptionally rare. I think you can get a lot of bells if you sell that fish. Are you sure you want to give it to me?"

"I'm sure. This would be a great fish to be on display in the museum. I can visit the fish every day and see it swimming in the tank," explained Alana.

Happy was still fixated on the piece of misinformation she had been told and wasn't paying attention to this bonding moment between Feathers and Alana. She wanted to know why she was told that Alana had to leave Furtopia.

"Feathers." Happy needed clarification. "You never asked Alana to leave the island? And you never spoke to Wayne, Tick, or Tock?"

"Never," replied Feathers as he placed the football fish in the tank and quietly admired the way it swam peacefully about.

There was a knock on the museum door. "Are you open?" a voice called out.

Feathers walked to the door and opened it. Lars was standing at the door. "I'm glad you're open. I thought you'd only be open during regular business hours."

"The museum isn't officially open yet," Feathers said, "but why are you here?"

"I was looking for Alana and she wasn't home. I was looking all over the island for her," explained Lars.

"I'm here," Alana called out.

"Oh good," Lars said as he walked into the museum. "I think there's been a big misunderstanding and I wanted to apologize."

"What type of misunderstanding?"

Lars paused. "I have to figure out the right way to explain it."

Happy interrupted, "You told me Alana was leaving the island."

Carl said, "You told me, too."

"Well, I guess the only way to explain it," said Lars, "is to say that I am a bit of a gossip. I've had issues like this before. I know it's bad, but I can't help telling juicy stories. I guess you can say I'm a storyteller, but then these are all excuses. I just want to apologize.

I didn't mean to tell everyone that you were leaving. When I told Happy and Carl the story about Feathers yelling at you, I embellished and said you were asked to leave Furtopia, and immediately regretted making this up—although it did make for a good story. It wasn't nice, and I can see that I caused all sorts of trouble. I've decided to leave the island because I don't think I deserve to be here."

"I accept your apology. We all make mistakes," said Alana. "I'm just glad I don't have to leave Furtopia."

Feathers said, "I should warn people that I am seriously afraid of bugs. If Alana had known that, I wouldn't have gotten so upset. Now you all know."

"Do you need to have bugs on display at the museum?" Alana questioned.

"Unfortunately," Feathers replied.

"I have a good idea. Why don't we place the wasp and firefly on display at the museum for you, so you don't have to deal with the bugs," suggested Alana.

"That's a great idea!" exclaimed Feathers.

"I volunteer to place all insects on the walls of the museum," said Lars, "and I hope this makes up for what happened."

Lars placed the wasp and firefly in the museum. Afterward, Feathers gave them a private tour.

CHAPTER 16

BUILDING BRIDGES

They left the museum when the sun was coming up. Lars suggested they watch the sunrise at the beach. Feathers joined them as they sat on the sandy beach and enjoyed watching the sun climb higher over the wavy water.

Alana said, "That's the first time I've watched the sun rise. It's beautiful."

"I love watching the sun rise and set. I also love watching the stars," said Lars. "I think you should place a telescope on the shore so we can all stargaze at night. I bet that would make the island more appealing to the judges."

With all the confusion surrounding the gossip-related chaos, Alana had almost forgotten about the contest. Although she had been heartbroken about the possibility of being asked to leave, a few positive things resulted from Lars's tall tale. Alana realized that Happy and Carl really did care about her and how much she wanted to stay on the island. She was also less focused on getting the island in shape for the contest and more focused on her friends. She'd be okay if Furtopia wasn't the prettiest island.

"I don't think we're going to win. We only have forty-eight hours left to prepare, and that's definitely not enough time," Alana said, "but I have a great idea. Instead of worrying about fixing up the island, I'd love to have you guys over for dinner tonight. I crafted a long dining table that has enough space for all of us. I could spend the day picking fruit and getting ready for the dinner. Doesn't that sound like fun?"

Happy said, "Forty-eight hours? That's two days. We have enough time if we work together. We can get the island in shape!"

"Do you really think so?" Alana asked skeptically.

"Of course. As you know, I work very fast. I can help," said Happy.

Alana knew Happy worked fast, but she also lost focus quite fast and she didn't have a great track record of following up on tasks. That said, Alana knew she should give Happy a chance. If Happy said she wanted to help, Alana should just accept that help.

"We should go to the store and buy a few items to help make the island pretty," suggested Alana.

When they reached the store, Carl asked if he could take a quick nap before he got to work. "You know, we were up all night and I am so tired."

"We were *all* up all night," Happy reminded him.

Lars said, "I have a lot of great ideas for making this island top rate and I can't wait to have you guys work on them."

"Lars!" Alana cried out, "you have to help, too!"

The group crowded into the store, and inquired about items like wallpaper for their homes, but Happy had to remind them that they were there to make the whole island pretty—not just their home's interior.

Wayne overheard them talking and said, "You won't even be considered if you don't build a bridge. There's an entire unexplored section of the island on the other side of the river, and you guys haven't been there because you don't have a bridge. You need to build a bridge together. I have a construction kit that is economical."

"Build a bridge?" Carl yawned. "That sounds like hard work."

"I'm up for it!" said Happy.

"Me too!" added Lars.

Feathers said he'd like to help, but Wayne reminded him that the museum was slated to open within twenty-four hours and as the museum director, it was his responsibility to see that it was ready for visitors. "Tick and Tock have been counting down the days to the grand opening," explained Wayne. "We can't have a delay. In fact, islands that don't have museums are also not in the running."

Feathers excused himself and went back to the museum while the gang carried the oversized construction kit to the river. Lars opened the box and Happy placed the pieces on the grass beside the river.

"There are so many parts!" Carl exclaimed. "This is going to take days."

Alana explained, "If we just take it one step at a time, we'll be fine."

"I hope so," Carl said as he flew across the river holding onto a wooden plank and placed it over the body of water. He continued to do this until all the wood was placed.

"Wow, you did such a great job," said Alana.

"Carl, flying saved us so much time," remarked Happy. "I wish I could fly. I would fly all day. I bet it's great cardio."

Alana was the first to walk across the bridge. "It's sturdy," she said. "We need to place the railing and then it's complete." Happy and Lars carefully put up the railing, and they all walked across the bridge.

Unfortunately, the uninhabited part of the island was overrun with weeds. Alana realized they had completely neglected that side of the island and there was a lot more work than she imagined. Happy declared, "I will make this island weed-free by the end of the day."

"I will plant flowers all over the island."

"I will build fences and create a pond on the old part of the island," said Alana.

"It's funny that you consider where we live to be the 'old part.' We just moved there a few days ago," Carl reminded her.

"I think we should break up into two groups. Alana and I will work on the part of the island with the houses and you can work on this fresh stretch of untouched land," Lars suggested.

Alana agreed. As she and Lars crossed the bridge, a balloon flew high above them carrying a white present wrapped in a red bow. Alana pulled out her slingshot and aimed for the balloon. Bullseye. The balloon fell to the ground and Alana pulled the present from the string and unwrapped it. She pulled out a clock. It was small and red and well-designed, like the heart-shaped wall clock she had coveted in the shop the other day.

"What a nice clock." Alana wondered where she should display it in her home, but Lars reminded her that they were running short on time and had much more to do.

CHAPTER 17

RAINY DAYS

They had twenty-four hours to make the island as pretty as they possibly could. Wayne told them that the judges were going to assess the island early the next morning. They'd be notified if they won and J. J. Swooner would play an intimate concert on Furtopia. Alana and Lars hummed their favorite songs while they created a large pond near the museum. Lars suggested placing a hammock and a bench near the pond.

"I like the idea that we can hang out by the pond as well as the beach. Adding a hammock and a bench will give people a reason to spend time here," Lars explained.

"You don't have to sell me on the idea. I think it's great. I loved the pond on your old island. I also love that people who either live in or visit Furtopia will have a place to sit beside the pond. I love how we took the best aspects of your island and brought them to Furtopia."

Lars agreed. He added, "I wonder who else might move to this island."

Alana thought of the many animal friends who

could join them. So far, they had a hamster, a chicken, raccoons, an owl, and a pig, but there were many other animal friends she had yet to make. While she worked, she thought about taking another trip to a mystery island. She had such a great experience meeting Lars and adding apples, coconuts, and a pond to Furtopia, and she wondered what else she could discover on future island explorations.

Once they created the pond, Alana felt a drop of water. At first, she thought it was fish splashing in the pond, but when a second and third drop dampened her face she looked up and saw dark clouds covering up the once-bright sky. A loud rumble shook the ground and a bolt of lightning lit up the now-gloomy and dark day.

"What should we do?" Alana asked Lars.

Alana was upset. They had so much work left to do, and they couldn't get it all done during a rainstorm, or could they? Lars pulled out two umbrellas from his pocket. He opened one of the red polka dot umbrellas and handed it to Alana.

"This should help."

"Thank you," Alana said, but within minutes she realized that it was impossible to garden, place a hammock, or carry a bench to the pond with an umbrella in one hand. The rain was going to slow them down and there was no way around it. Another bolt of lightning flashed in their direction and Alana screamed.

"I think we should go to your house and work on crafting furniture," said Lars. "This storm is intense."

They sprinted back to Alana's house where she crafted

a bench and also a set of wooden chairs to put beside the pond. "I feel like we're creating a park," she said to Lars.

"A park is a great idea. We can expand the garden we are planting beside the pond," suggested Lars.

As Alana worked, Lars spit out a ton of ideas to beautify Furtopia, and although all the ideas had merit, she was upset they couldn't complete any of them before the next morning. She looked out her window at the rain hitting the glass and heard the sound of thunder rattling her small house and she began to cry.

"This isn't fair! We were so close and now we're going to lose and we'll never hear J. J. Swooner live."

Lars said, "We can't let the rain get us down. I have an idea. Let's stop focusing on getting the island ready and let's go play in the rain." He walked to the window. "It seems as if the rain isn't as intense as it was before and there isn't any more lightning, so let's jump in the puddles and have fun!"

Alana dried her tears. "What a good idea!" she said. If life was going to throw her lemons, she was going to make lemonade. Alana and Lars didn't have rain slickers or umbrellas. They laughed as they raced to the beach, getting soaked and stopping to splash in every puddle on the way. When they reached the shore, Lars suggested they go fishing.

"I hear you find the best fish when it's raining," Lars informed Alana.

Alana pulled her rod from her pocket and began to fish. When she felt a tug, she reeled in a large fish. "What's this?" She held the long fish in her hand.

"I think that's a coelacanth," said Lars, "but we should bring it to Feathers for identification. If it is a coelacanth, it is one of the rarest fish you can find."

By the time they reached the museum, the sun had come out. Alana pointed to a large colorful double rainbow in the now blue sky dotted with clouds.

"Wow!" she exclaimed. "I don't know what will happen with the contest, but I can say that this is a truly beautiful island."

"I agree," said Lars.

Feathers walked down the museum steps and stopped to look at the double rainbow. "Do you know why double rainbows occur?" he asked, but Alana and Lars knew that was a rhetorical question and they stood patiently as Feathers lectured them on the science behind rainbows and why and when they occur. When he finished his mini lecture, Alana pulled out the coelacanth.

"What type of fish is this?" she asked.

"Oh my! Oh my! That fish is as rare as a rainbow. What a treat. You found a coelacanth. This will be the best museum grand opening ever. I can't wait to place it in the museum. Do you guys want to join me?"

"We'd love to, but we have a little more work to do," explained Alana. "We want to get the island in tip top shape before the judges make their decision."

"I understand," said Feathers, "but you guys can't miss my grand opening celebration tomorrow morning."

"We wouldn't miss it," Alana assured him.

They only had a few hours left to prepare and they had to get back to work.

CHAPTER 18

SINGING IN THE SUN

Alana woke up to the sun peering through the open curtains, but she didn't have the energy to get out of bed. She had stayed up most of the night trying to get the island in shape, leaving her exhausted despite having a few hours of sleep. There was another reason Alana didn't want to get up from bed: she was nervous about losing the competition. Would Furtopia be awarded the prettiest island certificate and would they be allowed to host a J. J. Swooner concert? She knew she couldn't spend all day in bed. She had to go the grand opening of the museum.

As she climbed out of bed, she let out a yawn. She put on a summer dress that she had purchased at the store. The pink floral pattern was colorful, and she wanted to dress up for the museum grand opening. She had never been to a grand opening before!

Once she was ready, she reached for the door handle just as there was a knock on the other side of the door.

"Alana!" Happy's upbeat voice called out. Although

Happy had worked alongside Carl and Lars until the wee hours of the night, she didn't appear tired.

"Are you ready for the grand opening?" Alana asked, stepping out onto the porch.

"Alana! Did you hear the news?"

Before Alana had a chance to answer, Carl and Lars sprinted toward the house. Alana couldn't believe tired old Carl was actually running.

"We won!" Lars screamed with joy. "We did it!"

"Seriously?" Alana's heart raced. This meant that J. J. Swooner, *the* J. J. Swooner would be arriving on their island that day and singing a private concert.

"Yes!" Happy said. "This is the best day ever."

"It is!" Alana agreed.

"J. J. Swooner is going to perform a concert on the beach following the museum's grand opening," said Lars.

This was exactly how Alana imagined it, so she was overjoyed. "Let's get going," she exclaimed, and the gang set out for the museum.

When they arrived, Feathers was already standing proudly on the steps of the museum while Wayne positioned himself at a podium placed in front of the museum. Wayne spoke about Feathers's dedication and his tireless efforts to get the museum ready for this auspicious occasion.

"Furtopia is now home to a world class museum, which will attract visitors from other islands. This museum will be filled with the greatest treasures found on Furtopia."

Everyone applauded. Feathers made a speech. "I'm so thrilled to be the director of this museum. I have to thank someone who was a great help to me. If it wasn't for Alana, the museum wouldn't have the many prized items you'll soon see on display. She deserves a round of applause."

Alana blushed. Wayne called out, "Alana should also be congratulated for developing this island. She did such a good job that in a few minutes the legendary J. J. Swooner will be performing on our shore."

At that moment, a seaplane flew low over Furtopia, creating a breeze. Alana looked up at the belly of the seaplane. "Can it be? Is that plane carrying J. J. Swooner?"

"I bet it is!" Lars called out in glee.

"Let's move the grand opening celebration to the beach," said Feathers, "and listen to the legendary J. J. Swooner belt out some sweet melodies. Perhaps he'll autograph his guitar and donate it to the museum."

"What a great idea!" Alana said, as the group raced to the dock just in time to see J. J. Swooner step off the plane with his guitar in hand and walk the few feet to the sandy ocean. He stood by the coconut tree and remarked, "This really is the prettiest island. I'm glad to be here."

Alana wanted to offer J. J. Swooner a tour of the island, but she didn't have a chance because within seconds of stepping onto the sand he started to strum his guitar and sing. His soulful, deep voice left the crowd cheering. They cried out for an encore, and

J. J. Swooner happily obliged. As Alana stood on the shore listening to J. J. Swooner's final song of the concert, she caught a glimpse of the smiles on her friends' faces, and when the song was over, she let out the loudest cheer.